Sabrina Sue
Loves the Sea

written and illustrated by
Priscilla Burris

Ready-to-Read

Simon Spotlight

New York   London   Toronto   Sydney   New Delhi

For Jeff, Siobhan, Lisa, Leslie, and Christina

SIMON SPOTLIGHT
An imprint of Simon & Schuster Children's Publishing Division
1230 Avenue of the Americas, New York, New York 10020
This Simon Spotlight edition May 2021
Copyright © 2021 by Priscilla Burris
All rights reserved, including the right of reproduction in whole
or in part in any form.
SIMON SPOTLIGHT, READY-TO-READ, and colophon are registered
trademarks of Simon & Schuster, Inc.
For information about special discounts for bulk purchases, please contact
Simon & Schuster Special Sales at 1-866-506-1949
or business@simonandschuster.com.
Manufactured in the United States of America 0321 LAK
2 4 6 8 10 9 7 5 3 1
Library of Congress Cataloging-in-Publication Data
Names: Burris, Priscilla, author, illustrator.
Title: Sabrina Sue loves the sea / written and illustrated by Priscilla Burris.
Description: New York : Simon Spotlight, 2021.
Audience: Ages 4–6. | Audience: Grades 2–3.
Summary: Little chicken Sabrina Sue lives on a farm but dreams of the sea,
and despite the other farm animals telling her she is ridiculous and silly,
she decides to set out on an adventure to finally see the ocean.
Identifiers: LCCN 2020042035 (print) | LCCN 2020042036 (ebook)
ISBN 9781534484245 (paperback) | ISBN 9781534484252 (hardcover)
ISBN 9781534484269 (ebook)
Subjects: CYAC: Chickens—Fiction. | Farms—Fiction. | Ocean—Fiction.
Classification: LCC PZ7.B5229 Sab 2021 (print)
LCC PZ7.B5229 (ebook) | DDC [E]—dc23
LC record available at https://lccn.loc.gov/2020042035
LC ebook record available at https://lccn.loc.gov/2020042036

Sabrina Sue was a little chicken with big dreams.

Sabrina Sue lived on a farm,
but she loved the sea.

She thought about the sea
her whole life.

She talked about the sea.

She sang about it every night.

I love the sea. Does it love me?

Her farm friends knew
she loved the sea.

Sabrina Sue did not mind being silly or foolish sometimes.

Now she wondered,
Should I stay, or should I go?

She made a plan and
packed her bag.

Early one morning, she
was ready.

She scrambled onto
Farmer Martha's truck

and hid in the haystacks.

The ride was bumpy.
The ride was bouncy.

She tumbled and toppled.

Farmer Martha's truck
stopped.
Sabrina Sue wondered,
Will I ever get to the sea?

She walked under tall trees.
She climbed over grassy
hills.

Then she saw it—
the sea!

It was even more beautiful
than in her dreams.
It seemed to go on forever.

The sand tickled her toes.

The salty air smelled fresh
and clean.

The seawater sparkled.

Sabrina Sue loved the sea.

But she began to miss
her farm friends.

And now she had stories
to share.

Sabrina Sue was happy to return to the farm.

But she knew she would visit the sea again someday!